W9-BRI-510

LEGO® DC COMICS SUPER HEROES

# JUSTICE LEAGUE VS BIZARRO LEAGUE

LOOK FOR LEGO®
DC COMICS SUPER HEROES:
JUSTICE LEAGUE VS. BIZARRO LEAGUE
AVAILABLE NOW ON DVD AND
BLU-RAY FROM WARNER HOME VIDEO

## SCRIPT WRITTEN BY MICHAEL JELENIC
## ADAPTED BY J. E. BRIGHT

SCHOLASTIC INC.

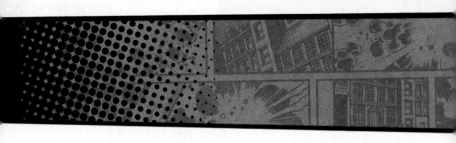

# CHAPTER 1: SUPERMAN'S TWIN?

**IT WAS A SUNNY DAY** at the playground in Metropolis. Children laughed as they raced around the equipment, playing on a merry-go-round shaped like an octopus. Their mothers chatted on benches at the edge of the sand, drinking coffee. Behind them in the parking lot was a line of identical SUVs.

The mothers sipped their coffees . . . and gasped as they spotted a blue blur whiz above the city, circling the golden globe atop the Daily Planet Building.

WEEEEE!

"Look!" the first mother shouted. "It's Superman!"

The being swooped down. He looked like a brutish, twisted version of Superman. The mothers screamed as the monstrous creature laughed harshly. Then he crash-landed, giggling, in the sand.

The children shrieked as they saw the scary thing laughing in the playground.

The messy monster became alarmed. He stared at the kids on the merry-go-round as they hollered in the octopus's spinning arms. "Bizarro save tiny people from tentacle creature!" he growled.

The kids screamed again as Bizarro barreled toward the twirling octopus. He yanked it free. Bizarro

grappled with the octopus, and children toppled into the sand. "No like calamari!" he hollered.

The mothers hopped, shrieking in alarm. Kids were crying everywhere.

Bizarro gave the roundabout a solid shake, and two kids flung free, sailing into the sky.

Another blur whooshed down toward the kids.

It was the real Superman!

He caught the children, gathering them safely in his grasp as he hovered. Superman lowered, easing the kids onto the sand.

The mothers sighed with relief as they saw their

children giggling next to Superman.

"Don't worry," said Superman. "They're just fine."

"Thank you, Superman!" cried his mother. "You saved my child from your crazy brother!"

"Oh no," said Superman, laughing awkwardly. "That's not my brother. It . . . I mean, *he* was created when Lex Luthor hit me with a duplicator ray."

Bizarro smacked the octopus roundabout hard against the blacktop.

"Excuse me," Superman said. He zoomed over. "Bizarro, put that down," he ordered.

"Bizarro put down," said Bizarro. He hurled the

octopus spinner overhead. It wheeled straight up until it vanished. He smiled proudly.

Superman rubbed his forehead. "*Down* means *up*. *Up* means *down*. Why does everything have to be backward with you?"

"Bizarro help Superman!" argued Bizarro, surprised. "Save Metropolis from tentacle creature!"

"Why is it every time you try to help," asked Superman, "Metropolis ends up destroyed? That octopus isn't a creature. It isn't even an octopus. It's not dangerous!" He sighed.

That was when the octopus merry-go-round returned to Earth. It slammed into the SUVs in the parking lot, smashing the vehicles into hundreds of tiny bricks. The SUVs broke into rubble, jumbling their pieces together in a heap.

"Ha-ha-ha," said Bizarro. "Boom!"

"My car!" a mother squealed. "Do you know how long it took me to assemble that? There were, like, so many bricks!"

Another mother pointed her finger at Superman. "Can you take your identical twin somewhere else?"

"Twins! Oh no," Superman said. "He's actually the opposite of me in every way."

Superman flew over to Bizarro.

"Bizarro save Metropolis!" Bizarro cheered.

"Bizarro save home!"

"You sure did," said Superman, shaking his head. Then he looked up into the sky. "You know," he told Bizarro, "I recently discovered a place that needs your help even more than Metropolis."

Bizarro's eyes blazed. "Let's not go!"

Superman nodded. "Follow me," he said, lifting off. "I mean"—he corrected himself—"*don't* follow me."

As Superman flew out of the playground and zoomed high above Metropolis, Bizarro kept close behind.

# CHAPTER 2: BIZARRO WORLD

**BIZARRO TRAILED SUPERMAN** up through Earth's atmosphere, past our solar system, and into the deep void of outer space.

Traveling at super-speed, they soon passed far-out stars into uncharted darkness.

Superman glanced at a handheld navigational computer. He studied the star charts.

"Should be around . . ." he muttered. Then he spotted what he was looking for. "*Ah*, right there."

A planet appeared as Superman and Bizarro flew toward it.

It was an enormous rocky cube floating in space.

Superman dived down, soaring into the cubic planet's atmosphere. Freaky lights flashed in the planet's clouds, shining in kaleidoscopic colors.

Both Bizarro and Superman gasped, startled, when the little computer in Superman's grasp suddenly fizzled and shattered, floating away in broken pieces.

Their entry through the atmosphere became more

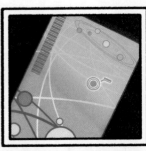

turbulent as they traveled toward the rocky surface below. Superman was badly shaken up. Bizarro giggled at the bouncy descent.

"Where you take Bizarro?"

"Somewhere you can't get into trouble," replied Superman. "This planet's physics are a little backward . . . just like you. It's going to be the perfect home."

Bizarro gazed out on the empty alien landscape. "Home Metropolis," he grunted. "How I save Daily Planet? How I save people here?"

"*Hmm*," said Superman, rubbing his chin. He

scanned the area, noticing the huge golden crystals dotting the desert. "Watch this." He carved crystals with his heat vision. Superman stacked the cut crystals until they resembled a jagged version of the Daily Planet Building with its signature globe. "Just like the one on Earth," he told Bizarro. "What do you think?"

Bizarro stared blankly at the teetering rocks.

With lasers from his eyes, Superman etched a simple smiley face on to a small crystal by the base of the rocky tower. Then he sliced a chunk of the globe

HE HE HE HE

THAT TICKLED!

and it slid down toward the smiley crystal below. "Bizarro!" called Superman. "That citizen is in trouble!"

Bizarro rocketed to catch the falling rock before it brained the stone citizen.

"You nothing to worry for, citizen," Bizarro said with a grin. "Bizarro keep safe." He patted the smiling crystal on the back. Its head popped off. "I think I kill him!"

Superman replaced the citizen's stone head. "He'll be just fine," he said. "He just needs to rest at home." His eyes gleamed with an idea. "Can you build him a home, Bizarro?"

HMM . . .

Nodding excitedly, Bizarro shouted, "Bizarro build!"

Superman hovered above the planet's severe surface. "I would wish you good luck, Bizarro," he said, "but you'd take it the wrong way."

He took off back toward Earth, leaving Bizarro alone in his new home.

# CHAPTER 3: GOING BANANAS

*ALL WAS QUIET* from Bizarro for a year.

In the meantime, Superman and his powerful friends in the Justice League stayed busy saving Metropolis.

One day the citizens ran screaming down the streets when the monstrous Giganta stomped across the city. With every thudding step she took, cars bounced. Giganta was eight stories tall and wore a leopard skin like a cavewoman.

Giganta shook the Daily Planet Building. "I got news for you!" she thundered. "Print is dead." With a mighty heave, she pushed the entire tower. The building slowly toppled.

Superman swooped in and caught the building. "This skyscraper is heavy." He pushed the building upright.

"Now Clark Kent doesn't have to look for a new job," Superman muttered. Giganta, scowling, raised her fist to punch Superman. A golden lasso circled her wrist.

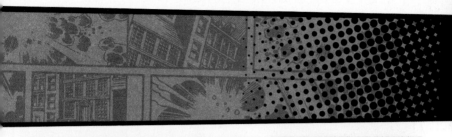

Wonder Woman yanked her lasso from where she stood atop her Invisible Jet. Giganta fell backward, plopping down with a thud. "Giganta, this is no way for a lady to act," scolded Wonder Woman. "Or dress. Animal prints are *so* last season."

"Leopard spots are the new black," replied Giganta. "And I'm going to make you black and blue!" She swung a vast fist.

Wonder Woman hovered out of the way on her jet. "If you say so!"

Giganta climbed back on her feet, punching at Superman and Wonder Woman as they ducked and fought around her.

Nearby, Gorilla Grodd stood on the ledge of a building. He wore his mind-control helmet. Gorilla Grodd smiled up at the rampaging Giganta.

"The perfect distraction for the perfect plan," he declared.

Grodd pressed a button on his helmet and telepathic energy waves circled out. He was controlling three villains—Deathstroke, the Penguin, and Captain Cold. Each carried crates out of a warehouse.

"The Justice League will never figure out what I'm really up to," hooted Gorilla Grodd.

"Let me take a shot at it," said Batman. He leaped between the gorilla and the villains. "You're using your

mind-control helmet to turn Giganta, the Penguin, Deathstroke, and Captain Cold into your henchmen. So while Giganta wreaks havoc on Metropolis you get your real prize."

"Pretty good guess," Grodd snarled. He reached up to press a button on his helmet.

Before he could touch it, a pair of rocket-powered metal hands snatched the helmet off the big gorilla's head. The hands carried the helmet back to their owner, Cyborg.

"Booyah!" Cyborg cheered. "Batman knew you'd try that. So he had me snatch your hypno-helmet." He crushed it in his fist. "He's just so smart."

The Penguin squawked as his brain cleared.

"Grodd had us under mind control."

Batman hurled another Batarang, which sliced the lid off a crate.

Dozens of bananas tumbled into the street.

"Nobody makes a monkey out of me," Deathstroke seethed. "Let's get out of here!"

While the villains scurried away, Grodd reached into another crate and pulled out a scary-looking weapon. He shot laser beams at Batman and Cyborg.

Batman flipped away from the deadly beams.

Gorilla Grodd opened the third crate, and put on the jet pack inside. He blasted into the sky.

Batman strapped on his own rocket-powered backpack. "Stay put, rookie!" he ordered Cyborg. He took off after Grodd, past where Giganta was squeezing Wonder Woman's Invisible Jet and Superman in her enormous fists.

The newest Green Lantern, Guy Gardner, arrived in a big green bubble floating over a nearby park.

AW, I WISH I HAD A JET PACK.

"Let me show you how a real hero does it!" he announced. He shined his power ring, creating a gigantic glowing copy of himself, which he could pilot from inside its head.

Wonder Woman rolled her eyes. "Wow, look, Superman," she said. "Guy Gardner finally made something as big as his ego."

Guy leaped at Giganta, but she was ready for him. "Say hello to the agony of defeat!" she shouted. Giganta kicked Green Lantern, connecting solidly

with her gargantuan foot.

Green Lantern tumbled backward and slammed upside down against a building. His giant creation fizzled, and he fell down and landed hard on his head. "Ow," he said.

At least he had distracted Giganta enough for Wonder Woman and Superman to gain the advantage in their battle with her.

Green Lantern and Superman buzzed around Giganta's head, and when she swung her fists at them, she tripped over the golden wire and fell over.

"Wrapping things up here," radioed Wonder Woman from her jet as she wrapped her lasso around Giganta's feet.

Using his power ring, Green Lantern created handcuffs big enough to hold her enormous wrists.

With Giganta under control, Superman contacted Batman. "How's it going with that big gorilla?" he asked. "Need any help?"

In their jet-pack chase, Batman whooshed after Gorilla Grodd, tossing Batarangs. "I don't need any help from you," Batman replied rudely.

Gorilla Grodd plunged through a pack of Boy Scouts, tumbling them into the air.

With lightning-fast reflexes, Batman hurled a dozen manacles, chaining the Boy Scouts together. He caught the whole matrix of scouts before they could fall. Then he took a shortcut, heading off Gorilla Grodd with the connected pack of Boy Scouts.

Gorilla Grodd got tangled in the scout chain. All the little boys clung to the gorilla, pummeling him

with their little fists.

Batman lowered the ball of Boy Scouts to the sand in the park, with Grodd unmoving in the middle. The scouts all cheered, and Batman pinned merit badges on their uniforms.

"Great takedown," Superman complimented Batman as he landed beside him. "But maybe next time, instead of using children to stop super-villains, call on your friends."

Batman narrowed his eyes and got into Superman's face. "I keep my friends close," he growled, "and my enemies closer."

"I hope not much closer than this," Superman joked. Then he realized how serious Batman was. "You're not implying that—"

Interrupting Superman, Cyborg leaped over and

started singing and dancing in victory, delighting the Boy Scouts.

"We caught Gorilla Groddy," Cyborg chanted, "and now we're going to party. Villains going to prison 'cause the Justice League is winning! Booyah!"

**THAT AFTERNOON,** the Justice League gathered around a big table in the Hall of Justice, their head-quarters.

Superman hovered at one end of the table. "Great work out there, everyone," he said. "Especially our two new recruits, Cyborg and Guy!"

Cyborg grinned at Batman. "The Man of Steel said I did great!" he cheered. "Fist bump!"

GREAT WORK OUT THERE, EVERYONE.

"I don't fist bump," said Batman.

"When we join forces, no evil can match us," continued Superman. "That's why we formed the Justice League. Together we fight for the liberties of all living creatures. I am proud of your individual accomplishments today . . ."

Batman's mind wandered during Superman's speech. *I joined the League to keep an eye on the most powerful being on Earth,* he thought. *The hearts and minds of man are no mystery to me. But an alien Superman . . .* Hidden from view, Batman pulled out a lead container. *Good thing I have my box of Kryptonite!* He opened it, and inside a chunk of space rock glowed.

Superman dropped to the floor.

Batman shut the box and hid it.

Groaning, Superman stood and glanced around uncertainly. "I'm okay," he grunted. "Not sure what came over me. I must have eaten some bad buffalo wings. Now where was I? *Ah*, yes. A hero sandwich sounds good." Cyborg followed Superman toward

the kitchen.

"Superman sure left in a big hurry," Batman growled suspiciously.

A loud alarm suddenly blared across the room.

Green Lantern, Wonder Woman, and Batman hurried over to the monitors.

"Great Hera!" cried Wonder Woman, studying the screens. "There are reports of Superman attacking LexCorp in Metropolis."

Batman pounded his fist into his glove. "Aha!" he said. "I knew he would snap one day! I tried to warn everyone, but no one would listen—"

Right then, Superman and Cyborg returned to the Great Hall, holding their lunches.

"*Uh*," said Cyborg, "we were just making sandwiches."

"Don't think I won't check that alibi," muttered Batman.

Superman peered at the monitor. "I have a pretty

good idea of who's behind this," he said nervously. "Why don't I take care of this one solo, guys?"

"I don't think so," replied Batman. "Let's go!"

Superman sighed, but he flew after his teammates as they rushed to the scene of the crime.

# CHAPTER 5: IN THE VILLAIN'S LAIR

**THE BATWING** and Wonder Woman's Invisible Jet landed outside the LexCorp tower in Metropolis. Superman and Green Lantern touched down near them. Cyborg rode with Batman.

A wide, ragged hole gaped in the wall of the building.

Superman chuckled unconvincingly. "Yeah, really, guys," he said. "I've totally got this."

"And miss all the action?" asked Cyborg. "Uh-uh." He ran toward the hole.

Superman sighed, and flew into the hole ahead of everyone else.

The Justice League followed Superman down

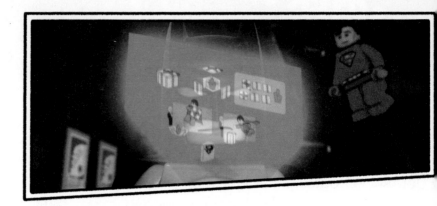

into a gloomy basement laboratory. Various weapons lined the walls in display cases.

"Is this a villain lair?" Cyborg squealed in excitement. "It's my first villain lair!"

By one wall, Batman discovered an open box with a cylinder inside. It was labeled as a Kryptonite bomb, and it included a hologram of plans for destroying Superman. "Lex has been busy plotting our demise," he said, peering at the plans.

Superman flew down beside him.

Batman turned off the hologram.

"Leave it to you to dispose of Lex's evil plans for me," said Superman.

"Yeah, that's what I was doing," said Batman.

"Took you long enough!" Lex Luthor hollered, running into the chamber. "My lab is destroyed!"

"Lex Luthor," Green Lantern sneered. "Do we

really have to help this guy?"

"What's that supposed to mean?" asked Lex sharply.

Superman glared at Lex. "You spend all day creating weapons to destroy us."

"How many times have you framed one of us for a crime," asked Batman, "and then run for president on a platform to stop us?"

Lex smiled. "That reminds me," he said, pulling out a stack of buttons, each printed with the words VOTE FOR LEX. He tossed them onto all the heroes' chests.

Behind them, Bizarro burst onto a high balcony.

"Bizarro!" cried Superman.

Batman tightened his hands to fists. "Another alien!" Cyborg glanced from Superman to Bizarro. "*Whoa*," he said. "Are you twins?"

Superman smacked his forehead. "We are not twins."

Then Superman noticed the weapon Bizarro held. "Great Scott!" he exclaimed. "The LexCorp duplicator ray that created you. You broke in here to steal it? Why?"

Bizarro raised the gun. "Bizarro show you."

"Don't!" shouted Superman.

Bizarro fired the ray. Superman flew out of the way, but the purple beam of energy hit Wonder Woman, Batman, Green Lantern, and Cyborg full blast.

The heroes grunted and groaned as they writhed in pain. They twisted as they were cloned, and collapsed onto the ground.

As Superman sat up, he blinked blearily . . . and

saw five creatures standing nearby.

The first looked like a wrong version of Batman. He turned his mask so it was on straight. "I Batzarro," he introduced himself. "World's Worst Detective."

"I am Greenzarro," said the next one. He whimpered, forming a teddy bear with his power ring, which he cuddled. "I scared."

A junky robot tottered forward. "I Cyzarro—" he said, and then slumped, fizzling. Bizarro flew behind him and turned the windup key in his back.

"I Bizarra," said the female creature. "Pretty, pretty princess."

"Bizarro," ordered Superman, "give me that ray before you do more damage."

"Nothing stop Bizarro!" hollered Bizarro. "Not even Superman!" He focused his freeze vision on the Justice League, encasing them in thick ice.

"Can we go?" whined Greenzarro. "I scared." He used his power ring to make a five-seat bicycle spaceship.

Bizarro noticed a cylinder in a case on the floor.

"*B-O-M-B*," he read. "Boom!" He grabbed it before hopping onto the bicycle spaceship. "Okay," he decided. "Let's stay!"

The rest of the Bizarro League hopped onto the bicycle and it streaked into outer space.

Superman melted the ice block with his heat vision, freeing the Justice League.

"That was weird," said Cyborg.

"How do we know this wasn't always part of your secret alien plan?" asked Batman.

"Because Bizarro can't keep secrets," Superman answered. "He can barely keep his pants up."

"Why make duplicates of us?" wondered Wonder Woman.

"I don't know," replied Superman, "but if one Bizarro can cause this much destruction, think what an entire Bizarro League can do. I know where they've gone: Bizarro World. Let's go!"

As Wonder Woman, Green Lantern, and Cyborg followed Superman out of the lab, Batman hung back.

"So," Batman murmured, "you want us to follow you to some distant planet. Well, I'll play your little game for now, alien."

Then Batman hurried to catch up with his team-mates.

# CHAPTER 6: BIZARROTROPOLIS

**SUPERMAN AND GREEN LANTERN** traveled through space on their own power. Wonder Woman flew in her Invisible Jet, and Batman and Cyborg took Batman's spaceship. They reached Bizarro World in the far reaches of the galaxy.

"Merciful Minerva!" cried Wonder Woman. "Bizarro's planet is a cube?"

"I should warn you," said Superman, "things here behave a little—"

"*Um*," Wonder Woman interrupted, "bizarro?"

Batman's spaceship shuddered and shook. Wonder Woman's jet vibrated uncontrollably, too. Both vehicles shattered into tiny bricks.

Cyborg, Batman, and Wonder Woman plummeted toward the surface.

"One rescue rocket coming up," said Green Lantern. He concentrated, but his power ring created a big green

MERCIFUL MINERVA!

chicken instead.

"A chicken," said Batman as they landed. "How degrading."

"I call that use of power ring a clear foul," joked Cyborg. "Get it? Fowl?"

With a scanner, Batman studied a gold crystal. "These rocks are emitting a weird form of radiation."

"We should call it *weirdiation*," said Cyborg. "I like that name!"

Batman shot Cyborg an annoyed glance. "It's this radiation—"

"I do not know what you're talking about," Cyborg said. "Radiation? There are so many kinds."

"Fine," seethed Batman. "It's this *weirdiation* that created the planet and is now interfering with the team's powers and equipment."

"Equipment?" Cyborg peered down at his body, worried. "That's what I'm made of—" His arm fell off.

"Hey," Green Lantern asked Superman, "why

doesn't this place affect you?"

"Well, not much does, I guess," Superman replied.

Batman eyed Superman suspiciously. *So*, he thought, *the Kryptonian lured us to a planet that renders our powers and weapons useless. Well, I have something that will affect him.* Batman patted his secret box of Kryptonite.

Then Batman froze. He hid the box. "*Shh*," he hissed. "We're being watched." He rolled on the ground stealthily, before popping up beside a

figure on a rocky ridge. "What do you want?" Batman demanded.

Green Lantern flew over. "I think he wants to know why you're talking to a rock."

Batman narrowed his eyes. Now it was obvious that the figure was crudely formed from crystal.

"It's a citizen," explained Superman. "I tried to make this place feel more like home for Bizarro."

From the ridge where they stood, the Justice League now could see a vast city. It looked like

Metropolis, but warped and weird, and filled with crystal citizens. "It's Bizarrotropolis," said Cyborg. "I like making up funny names."

Superman's smile faded when he heard the sounds of a distant battle. "I'm going to investigate."

"Not without me, you're not," said Batman. As Superman flew off, Batman snagged the corner of his cape and hitched a ride.

With a glance back, Superman asked, "Beautiful from up here, isn't it? Oh . . . unless you want us both to fall and become pancakes, I'd keep your lead box full of Kryptonite closed tight . . . *Bruce Wayne*."

"Ha!" cried Batman. "I knew you'd use your X-ray vision on me! But how did you see through my lead-lined mask?"

"I didn't," replied Superman, "but somebody stitched your name onto the elastic band of your underwear."

"Alfred," grumbled Batman.

Superman smiled. "You can trust me with your secret identity. I'm Superman!"

"I don't trust anyone," said Batman. "Also, you're an invulnerable alien whose motives remain mysterious, which means I should especially not

trust you . . . *Clark Kent*."

"Hey," protested Superman, "how did you know my secret identity?"

Batman smiled. "I'm Batman."

Superman slowed for a landing on an outcropping. He and Batman witnessed a surprising scene in the wide valley below.

"That's the source of the sound I heard earlier," said Superman.

An enormous space destroyer floated above the plain. The front of it was shaped like the giant, familiar head of a villain. Behind the destroyer was a hopper filled with golden crystals. Bolts of electricity snaked out of the sides, hoisting more crystals into the ship.

"Darkseid," Superman and Batman said in unison.

# CHAPTER 7: TICKLED TO DEATH

**THE BIZARRO LEAGUE** rushed to the scene, battling to stop the ship from grabbing the rocks.

"Must not save citizens from big head machine!" bellowed Bizarro.

Bizarra pulled rocks back with her lasso, while Greenzarro blocked levitation beams with teddy bears. Batzarro and Cyzarro saved citizens, too.

Inside the destroyer's control room, Darkseid sat on a throne. "Who is stealing my rocks?" he demanded of his henchman Desaad who was working the ship's controls.

"No one, Master Darkseid," Desaad assured his boss. "This is only a minor interference." Desaad

peered at a monitor. "Unleash the drones!"

A horde of drones detached from the destroyer and whizzed toward the Bizarro League.

The drones blasted the Bizarros with lasers, knocking them to the dirt.

"It tickle!" cried Batzarro, giggling.

Up on the outcropping, Superman asked, "They're being tickled?"

"Tickled to death," growled Batman.

Batman and Superman leaped into the fray, smashing drones into scattered bricks.

Inside the ship, Desaad gasped. "Superman?"

"Superman is here?" hollered Darkseid.

"And Batman," Desaad replied. "They have unexpectedly joined forces."

"Crush them," ordered Darkseid.

Down below, Superman and Batman freed the Bizarro League from the tickle attack, and they all fought the drones together.

Superman gasped as he spotted a vast boulder flung from the destroyer.

The boulder smashed down atop the heroes, flattening the area completely.

With the heroes crushed, the ship picked up the remaining crystals in the valley. Then it headed toward the horizon to find more rocks.

When the second the destroyer left, Superman spun upward from a tunnel in the ground. Batman and the Bizarro League climbed out.

"Good thinking," Batman told Superman. "Creating a tunnel saved us all."

Superman grinned. "Was that a compliment?"

Green Lantern carried Wonder Woman and Cyborg into the valley on green chickens.

Batman greeted his teammates. "We're dealing with something big now."

"Darkseid," said Superman.

SUPERMAN?

CRUSH THEM.

Wonder Woman and Green Lantern gasped.

"I'm guessing that's a bad thing?" asked Cyborg.

"Oh, he's just the most dangerous force in the universe," replied Green Lantern.

"Is that why you stole the Bizarro ray and created your own league?" Superman asked Bizarro. "To stop Darkseid?"

Bizarro nodded. "Bizarro wanted to protect his citizens from big head machine."

"We can help you," said Superman.

"*Whoa!*" Green Lantern warned. "Easy for you to say, Mr. I've-Still-Got-My-Powers."

"Are you scared, Guy?" Wonder Woman teased.

"Why risk our behinds for meaningless rocks, Princess?" replied Green Lantern.

Bizarro hung his head. "Rocks my only friends

after Superman send me away."

"I sent you here because—" began Superman.

"Because you embarrassed by Bizarro!" Bizarro interrupted. "So you hide him."

"They may just be rocks," Batman broke in, "but I suspect Darkseid wants to harvest their unique properties for a weapon."

"Harnessing their power could render Earth's defenses useless," added Wonder Woman.

"If Darkseid is after these rocks," said Superman, "then he's headed to the greatest concentration of them."

WHOA!

The Justice and Bizarro Leagues rushed to Bizarrotropolis.

"I have a plan," said Batman. He pointed at the pieces of his spaceship and the Invisible Jet. "I'm going to reconstruct the blocks of these vehicles to create a thermodynamic amplifier of the Bizarro ray. When fired at Darkseid's weirdiation supply it will create a new opposite form of matter, and the two will annihilate each other, destroying his ship."

The Bizarros blinked blankly at Batman.

Greenzarro held his head. "All I hear is, 'blah, blah, blah, science, blah, big word.'"

Batzarro raised his hands. "I have better plan," he announced. "First we take nap!"

The Bizarros all cheered that suggestion . . . and conked out.

"I think we should go with Batman's plan," said Wonder Woman.

# CHAPTER 8: THE KRYPTONITE BOMB

**IN THE CITY,** Superman found Bizarro sitting alone with a crystal citizen. "Something bothering you?"

"On Earth I bad hero," Bizarro explained. "On Bizarro World I bad hero. All I want is save the day like Superman." He patted the citizen's shoulder, and its head slid off.

Superman turned the citizen's head over. "The Justice League will save the day, Bizarro. I promise."

After Superman flew off, Bizarro took out Lex Luthor's bomb. "No," he whispered. "Bizarro save day."

At the edge of the city, Darkseid's destroyer collected its crystals.

Superman swooped down to Wonder Woman,

BAD HERO.

BIZARRO SAVE DAY.

Green Lantern, and Cyborg. "We've got to buy Batman some more time. Let's go!"

In the destroyer, Desaad gasped at the heroes' return. "This is going to make you laugh," he told Darkseid. "Nobody was crushed. Please don't hurt me."

"I will deal with them myself," said Darkseid. He rose on a platform to a hatch on top of the destroyer. He launched a new battalion of drones.

Wonder Woman, Bizarra, Bizarro, Green Lantern, and Greenzarro fought the drones while Superman flew up to face Darkseid.

Bizarra fell into a fighting frenzy, pummeling

drones and tearing them apart.

"By Athena's gray eyes," cheered Wonder Woman, "she is a dog of war!"

"Then why is my guy such a pussycat?" asked Green Lantern. Greenzarro cowered nearby, afraid to challenge the drones.

"Why can't you be more like her?" Green Lantern asked, pointing at Bizarra.

Greenzarro shrugged, hiding behind a citizen.

"You can do it!" shouted Green Lantern. "I believe in you! You're a Lantern."

Then a squadron of drones whizzed at Green Lantern. He raised his ring to zap them but it fizzled. "Still not working," he moaned. The drones buzzed in.

"No!" screamed Greenzarro. He leaped in front of Green Lantern and raised his ring, creating a giant teddy bear around them both.

The drones bounced off the teddy bear, crashed into each other, and exploded.

While working on building a ship, Batman glanced up at the battle. "They better watch for Darkseid's Omega Beams."

"What's an *Omega Beam*?" asked Cyborg.

Darkseid shot luminescent rays from his eyes at Superman.

Superman dodged the beams, but they followed him like heat-seeking missiles. The rays zapped Superman, smashing him into the side of a hill.

"Those are Omega Beams," said Batman.

Superman shook off the painful attack, and zoomed back up to the destroyer to fight Darkseid.

"We'll never let you harness the power of this planet, you space bully!"

"I will," Darkseid swore. "And after Earth falls the entire universe will bow to me!" He tossed Superman off the destroyer.

Superman crash-landed near Batman.

"I need more time, Superman," Batman said calmly.

Nodding, Superman struggled to fly back into battle.

Cyzarro and Batzarro impatiently watched Batman and Cyborg working on the ship.

"I can break for you," Cyzarro offered.

Cyborg shook his head. "That's what we're worried about."

Batzarro grunted in frustration, then shoved Cyborg and Batman out of the way. "Cyzarro, break now!"

Cyzarro hurtled over Cyborg, and punched his arm into the ship's console. A wave of electricity shot up his arm, blasting everyone off their feet.

But the ship's engine began to hum.

"He fixed it," Batman said, amazed.

"Of course," Cyborg realized. "Only a Bizarro can make technology work here."

Batman hopped in the cockpit, piloting the ship toward the destroyer.

Meanwhile, Superman redoubled his attacks against Darkseid, punching the villain repeatedly to little effect. Darkseid grabbed Superman again and hurled him against a wall atop the destroyer. "*Oof*," said Superman. "Not fun."

"You're too late, Superman," said Darkseid. "I now have enough of this bizarre energy to rule the galaxy."

Superman groaned, stumbling back onto his feet. "Well," he said bravely, "on Bizarro world, rules are meant to be broken."

Darkseid turned around.

Batman hovered behind him in his new ship, ready to fire.

OOF.

"Bizarro save day!" screamed Bizarro, jumping in front of Batman's ship. He hurled Lex Luthor's cylindrical bomb at Darkseid.

It exploded in a blast of bright-green energy.

Superman yelled as he fell off the destroyer, tumbling down on the rocks below.

Batman's ship exploded into pieces. Luckily, he was able to eject in time.

But Darkseid was unhurt. He smiled at Bizarro. "A Kryptonite bomb," he said. "Thank you." He lowered himself down into his destroyer and sat on his throne.

"Desaad," said Darkseid, "let us test our weapon on Earth."

## DESAAD PRESSED A BUTTON.

A cannon poked out of the top of the destroyer, and fired a massive beam of power.

It zapped the moon, transforming it into a cube.

Then the beam whizzed toward Earth.

Suddenly, a ship soared soared into the ray's path. It was Hawkman! "Hawk jet, inbound!" he shouted. "Deploying hawk swords! Pressing hawk button!"

A multitude of giant glowing swords swirled around the jet, forming a vast bird of purple energy that blocked the beam.

"Hawkman," Batman called over the radio, "did you manage to intercept the ray?"

Hawkman's jet shook so badly it felt like it might explode. "You could say that."

Back on Bizarro World, the Justice and Bizarro Leagues gathered around the fallen Superman.

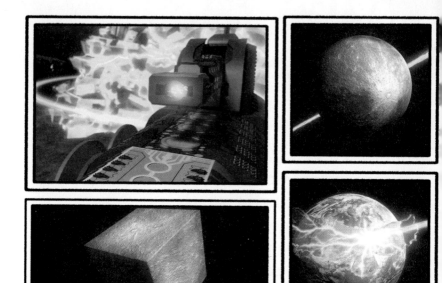

"Hawkman is holding off the ray," Batman reported to the group, "but I suspect his armor will eventually fall to the weirdiation."

"Bizarro tried to help," sobbed Bizarro.

"Yeah, you helped, all right!" Green Lantern yelled. "You helped Darkseid! Thanks to you, Earth is toast! Without Superman, we can't stop him."

"Yes," moaned Superman. "Yes, you can."

Everyone moved closer to hear Superman's weak voice.

"Darkseid's ship is somehow being protected

from the weirdiation," whispered Superman, "but if we overload the ship with those crazy rocks . . ."

Batman threw up his hands. "But that'll just make his weapon stronger," he said. "So this is how you destroy us all!"

Superman met Batman's eyes. "You need to trust me."

"Trust you?" said Batman. He turned away, biting his lip, squeezing his hands to fists.

Finally, Batman let out a long breath. "Well . . ." he said, "if there's one place I can try trusting you, it's on a backward world."

Bizarro pointed to the crystals. "No!" he cried. "Those are Bizarro's people! His friends."

WE CAN'T STOP HIM!

"I know, Bizarro," said Superman. He waved his hand at the other Bizarros. "But you have new friends now . . . and an old one, too."

Bizarro's mouth dropped open. "Superman Bizarro's friend?"

"Not just friends, Bizarro," Superman said sincerely. "*Brothers*. I should have been a better one to you."

Bizarro grinned. "Twin brothers?"

Superman nodded. "Fraternal, but yes. Twins."

Bizarro grunted happily. Then he marched into his city and tossed his crystal citizens into the hopper of Darkseid's destroyer.

"Good-bye," sobbed Bizarro. "Bizarro miss you."

Greenzarro, Bizarra, Batzarro, and Cyzarro joined Bizarro in throwing citizens into the destroyer's hopper. The Justice League helped, too.

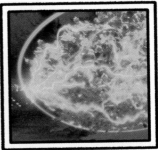

"I miss you!" Bizarro told another crystal citizen before hurling him up into the enormous pile. Bolts of electricity shot through the hopper, crossing over into the ship as the crystals overloaded the systems.

Fireballs exploded along the destroyer's sides.

A huge blast launched the head-shaped cockpit into deep space, hurtling Darkseid far away from Bizarro World.

Across the galaxy, Hawkman had nearly lost his struggle to keep the beam from reaching Earth. "Must keep pressing button! So hard!"

Then the ray fizzled out.

Hawkman started to celebrate . . . but the moon was still a cube.

On Bizarro World, the Justice League and Bizarro League waited for Batzarro to examine Superman.

"Superman A-OK," announced Batzarro.

"That's great," said Cyborg. "He's going to be all right, then?"

"No," replied Batman. "Batzarro means we can't save him."

Wonder Woman lowered her head. "Good-bye, Kal," she whispered.

Bizarro stood next to Superman. "Superman live."

"Stop with the opposite talk, man!" cried Cyborg.

Bizarro shook his head. "No. Superman live!" He

sucked in a deep breath, inhaling the glowing Kryptonite radiation from the Man of Steel. As Superman's complete opposite, Kryptonite was totally harmless to him. Bizarro let out a big burp.

Superman raised his head. "You . . ." he muttered, "saved the day, Bizarro."

Bizarro grinned as his friends slapped him on the back. "Bad job!" cheered Batzarro.

Batman kneeled beside Superman. "I'm not wrong often," he admitted, "but I was about you. You can be trusted."

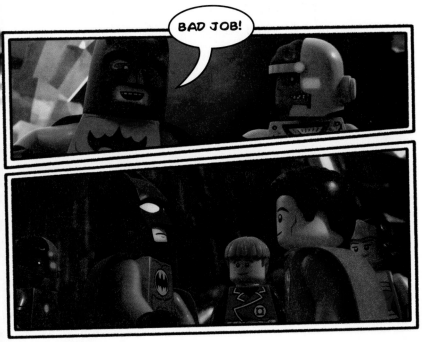

"Really?" Superman asked. "Then I guess you won't need that box of Kryptonite anymore."

"Let's not go crazy," said Batman.

Superman climbed shakily to his feet. "Well, if we're going to have a wildcard on the team who keeps tabs on me, I'm glad it's you," he told Batman. He stared at the wrecked landscape. "*Whoa*, look at this place."

Bizarro heaved a big sigh. "Bizarro lost whole world."

"Then we're going to have to rebuild it together," declared Superman.

Both the Bizarro League and the Justice League put their combined efforts into rebuilding the strange civilization on Bizarro World.

"Great job!" said Superman, looking around at the crystal construction. "In fact, the whole place looks wonderful. I can't wait to walk through that front door."

"*Hmm*," said Bizarro. "Front door."

THE-EN